Santa's Stocking Stuffers
By
Andrea Smith (writing as Laurel Landon)
Copyright © 2017

Table of Contents

acknowledgments

TO SANTA CLAUS, AND to the magic of Christmas!

Prologue

Sometimes the holidays are more hype than reality. Have you ever noticed that? You can't escape the commercials on television, depicting happy families opening their presents Christmas morning, steamy cups of hot cocoa on the table in the background.

Or what about the Santas on every corner, ringing a bell, waiting for passersby to drop some cash into the black pot hanging from a tripod next to them?

And you can forget about going into any store after Halloween if you'd just rather forget the whole Christmas brouhaha... Not going to happen.

The piped in Christmas carols chiming through the overhead sound system, aisles overstuffed with Christmas paraphernalia. The smells of gingerbread and pumpkin spice wafting from the bakery section triggering those happy holiday memories from childhood.

And the toy aisles. Crammed with pushy shoppers elbowing one another to get that last bargain Barbie, or stepping on each other's feet to grab the 'limited supplies' on the latest Nintendo game.

It's an emotional time for many. A time where budgets are strained, memories of past Christmases aren't particularly happy ones, and real life has been so tragic that not even a Big Mart Santa can cheer them up.

But sometimes he just has to try.

My name is Nick. And from the day after Thanksgiving - commonly known as "Black Friday" - until Christmas Eve I am a Wal-Mart Santa. And I'd like to think the package I deliver in some small—or big way—-help those needing it most.

You see, I know how to find the ones most in need. It's a gift. It's one of the reasons why I do it. The money is crap, but it's not about the money for me. It's about giving of myself to someone who is appreciative of the connection I offer.

This year I want to share with you just how much joy I spread for those needing that special something to bring them out of their holiday melancholy.

Chapter 1

"SONYA"

December 15th

I hate this time of year. If I could have some sort of an anesthesia drip at my disposal from Thanksgiving to January 2nd every year, it's what I would do. I would simply crawl into bed in my favorite plaid flannel pajamas, pull my comforter up and under my chin, and sleep away until the New Year has come and gone.

It hasn't always felt this way for me. Only the last two years. Ever since I caught Richard on top of my best friend Linda, his naked ass bucking up and down as he plunged his dick into her.

Yep. Happened at a Christmas party we were hosting for our friends and co-workers. He blamed the alcohol; I blamed his horniness and total lack of character. We'd only been married for six friggin' months at the time.

Now they were married. Linda was due to deliver their first child between now and Christmas. What a great present for Richard. One I know he always wanted; one that I should have been able to give him if given half a chance.

At this very moment I'm in a freaking over-crowded Wal-Mart, looking for the bargain 12 rolls of toilet paper for $4.99 Christmas special. Jesus Christ—-I need a life.

I rise to my tip toes to grab one of the last ones when my fingers brush against it, missing. It teeters on the edge of the shelf, and then topples down, hitting me squarely in the face. "Damn!" I sputter, stepping back, my butt unceremoniously ramming into somebody else's shopping cart with a thud.

I bend down to pick up the toilet paper when a familiar voice sounds behind me. "Sonya? Are you okay?"

And there she is. Linda. Big belly protruding out from her coat, face lit up with the glow of pregnancy, and a big fat diamond sparkling from her left hand as she brushes her dark locks back from her face.

"Oh hell no," I mutter, turning on my heel and making tracks down the aisle and around the corner, ignoring Linda calling after me. "I'm sorry, Sonya, we just fell in love. Can't you understand that? It . . . happens!"

"Why me?" I hiss to nobody. This is so not fair. A sob escapes me, coming from somewhere foreign, because I truly am not a crybaby. Her words echo over and over again in my head:

We fell in love . . .

We fell in love . . .

Fuck them and their love! When did Richard *fall out of love* with me? I thought back. There had been no signs. Nothing to tip me off that he and I weren't happy. How stupid and clueless had I been?

The sad thing is that I hadn't been with a man since Richard left. It had destroyed me. He had destroyed me. I had no shred of confidence left. I'd ordered tons of Chinese take-out, crawled into our bed and watched Lifetime Movies through the rest of December and well into January. I'd lost my job, and got evicted from our apartment. In the process, I'd gained twenty pounds.

My mother had tried to help. She told me to cry; to grieve, and then let it go and move on with my life. But I didn't want to cry. It was a sign of weakness to cry—-at least that's what my father had always preached.

So I simply ignored her advice. Moved in with her until I could find another job, and continued to eat Chinese takeout. I was embarrassed about my weight gain. I'd let myself go, there was no denying that, so it was my excuse for not trying to cultivate a new relationship with the men I came into contact with at my job or through social gatherings.

But now the tears won't be denied; it was too much just now coming face to face with Linda. I grab the packaged rolls of toilet paper from my cart and rip the plastic at the top, grabbing the top roll and unwinding a large length. I bury my face into it, trying to muffle my sobs as other shoppers walk by giving me quizzical looks and pathetic stares.

Oh fuck them. Fuck everybody!

How did you spend your Christmas holiday, Sonya?

Oh, I had this super cool meltdown in the house wares aisle at Wally World, how about you?

I quieted my sobs and was blowing my nose when I felt a hand on my shoulder. If this was Linda I just might sucker punch her, pregnant or not. I turned quickly and looked up into the warm, incredibly blue eyes of the Big Mart Santa.

"Excuse me miss," he said, his voice smooth and soft, "Is there anything Santa can do to help you?"

I shake my head vehemently. This was the epitome of humiliation. I was twenty-nine years old and had garnered the attention of a discount store Santa Claus as he observed me sobbing and snorting into a big wad of toilet paper I hadn't even paid for yet.

"Oh . . . I . . . I'm just having a moment," I reply, "It's just . . . well, holidays *suck* *if* you want to know the truth. No offense, Santa."

He smiles a genuine smile, and I can tell that Santa isn't much over thirty himself. Straight white teeth, and despite the fluffy white beard and moustache, that masks his face, I can see that there are no crinkle lines around his eyes. His brows are dark brown.

"Would you like to tell Santa about it? It's not just about what you'd like for Christmas. It's also about how you feel about Christmas. That's why I'm here."

"Oh . . . oh I couldn't . . . you have kids to see——"

"Nobody here right now," he replies, nodding towards the empty plush red chair surrounded by big plastic elves that are lit up around the fake Christmas tree. "Won't you come into Santa's Village and tell him all about it? What's your name little girl?"

"Sonya," I reply meekly.

"Well, Sonya, I'd really like to hear your story. You never know, Santa may be able to help."

I'm dubious, but something inside my head whispers 'why not?' What can it possibly hurt to unload to somebody else. Maybe a fresh perspective.

And so I did. I couldn't actually believe I did it, but there was something so sincere and engaging about this guy, I found myself sitting on his lap and spilling my guts to him about the past year. I spared nothing. I told him about my weight gain, my job loss, my penchant for Chinese takeout and Lifetime

Movies - and the fact that I hadn't had sex for more than a year now. Somehow, I hadn't felt ashamed in admitting that to him. After all, he was Santa, right? He'd likely heard it all before I decided.

"Well, now Sonya, it sounds as if you have every reason to hate the holidays. That makes Santa kind of sad though. Let's see what I can do to fix that for you." He reaches behind his chair and pulls out a huge black silk bag. I watch in wonderment as he gropes through it, finally pulling out a small felt stocking that had some candy poking out of it. If he thinks a Tootsie Pop and licorice are going to heal the wound , I'm actually sorely disappointed in his *Santa* abilities.

My face drops and he catches it. I hear a soft chuckle rumble from beneath his snowy white beard. "Make sure you get everything out of the stocking. Santa thinks maybe there's something special in it just for Sonya."

I give him a smile, lifting myself off of his lap. "Thanks, Santa. I will."

I check out at the front register, and as I'm pushing my cart towards my car in the lot, I pull the stocking from my pocket, deciding to go for the Tootsie Pop since it's well past dinner time.

Once my car is loaded up with my groceries and staples, and I'm in the driver's seat sucking on my pop, I empty the rest of the stocking out onto the passenger seat. Licorice, two chocolate kisses, and a folded up piece of paper tumble out.

I grab the paper up, quickly unfolding it. My sucker drops from my mouth and onto my lap as I read the words:

Meet me at the Motel 6 on Branson Road near the freeway exit. Room 232. Anytime after 10:00 pm. I have something you want. Something you need.

Is this what I think it is? A bootie call? A bootie call from . . . *Santa?*

No . . . can't be. Can it? Am I brave enough to show up? How do I know he doesn't pass these things out to every chick crying her eyes out in the house wares aisle at Big Mart? No way will I show up. This is just plain crazy.

Or is it?

I think about it momentarily using some female logic. Maybe it is just what I need. A hook-up with a stranger. A stranger that already knows my sad story; who will forgive me if I turn out to be a bumbling idiot in the sack.

No judgment.

No expectation.

No strings.

At 10:30 p.m. there I stand in front of Room 232 at the Motel 6 and my hand hesitates only a few seconds before I collect my nerve and knock. From inside I hear the sound of the television going, and then the lock clicks and the door opens.

It's Santa. Only now he's wearing jeans and a black tee that fits snugly, showing off a great build. His hair is dark brown, a little longer than most guys are wearing, but it's wavy and well kept. A bit of five o'clock shadow is showing, which gives him a rakish appeal. His feet are bare, and I can tell he's fresh out of the shower. Like me.

"Santa?" I ask tentatively.

"Yes, Sonya, it's me. Please come in."

I step inside and immediately my mind goes to the darkest of places. What if he's "psycho Santa?" Some kind of sociopathic murderer? What if this is the last place I see before I die?

"Would you care for some eggnog? I bought some in hopes you might want to share a beverage with me this evening."

"Umm . . . sure, I guess," I reply as he helps me off with my jacket. His eyes peruse me, and I flush under his gaze.

"I like a lady with some curves, and my sweet Sonya, you've got them all in the right places. You are simply beautiful," he says huskily, walking past me to where he's got glasses set out on the desktop. He pours eggnog into each glass, and then puts a shot of rum into each, stirring them.

I down mine quickly, wanting the rum to take the edge off of my nerves. "Umm . . . am I supposed to keep calling you Santa?"

He takes a slow swallow of his drink and then smiles. "You can call me Nick. Now, turn around for me, and start taking off your clothes. I need to feast my eyes on you and your lovely curves Sonya."

I do as I'm told, moving slowly because quite frankly, I'm still not totally convinced this guy isn't a psycho, or at the very least a whack job, but what the hell, it's time I took a walk on the wild side. Nothing ventured, nothing gained and all that crap, right?

In seconds, I hear the sound of his zipper, followed by the sound of his jeans falling in a heap at his feet. I turn back around just as he steps out of them, his eyes still on mine, as I pull my sweater up and over my head. We're now standing at the foot of the bed.

"What are you waiting for? Don't you want to see what you've been wondering about since you first walked into my room?"

I feel warmth flood my cheeks as I peer down and see his impressive erection flat against his belly. No boxers. No tighty-whities.

Nick goes commando.

And that's pretty freakin' hot. Then I notice the glint of silver.

Oh wow. His dick is pierced.

Oh. My.

I squirm a bit at the thought of having a dick with jewelry attached inside of me. I clear my throat. "Aren't you gonna take your shirt off?" I ask, as if I've seen a zillion pierced cocks of his generous size. I mean, come on! No sense in giving Santa a big head, right?

No pun intended.

"Whatever you want, Sonya," he replies, taking both hands and pulling his shirt up and over his head. I view his broad chest, and admire the corded muscles of his upper arms. My gaze lowers to his firm flat belly, and the narrow line of dark hair that trails south to what he's got hanging "Now, your turn, Sonya. I want to watch you finish undressing. And I want you to take it nice and slow for my viewing pleasure."

I release the breath I've been holding, and give a slight nod of acknowledgement.

He backs up the few steps to where the king-sized bed starts, and lowers himself onto it, rolling to his side, one leg propped, one arm crooked, and his head resting on his hand. His eyes don't waver and I can see he expects me to do exactly as he's instructed.

What the hell?

I can do this.

I will do this.

I lean over and remove my boots first, along with my socks. I straighten up and unclasp my front closure bra, releasing my tits for his viewing pleasure. I let my bra drop to the floor, and take this opportunity to cup my own breasts with my hands. I slowly massage them in a circular motion; my tongue wets my lower lip as he continues to watch what I'm doing.

I lick my index and middle finger, and then move them back to a breast, where I bring my nipple to full erection. I don't miss the fact he's moved his free hand to his cock, gripping it and slowly stroking it while watching me.

My fingers move to my other breast and I gently rub and tease that nipple, allowing a soft moan to escape. His eyes darken from blue to a dark stormy grey, and his tongue flickers across his lower lip.

I move one hand to the waistband of my jeans, slowly freeing the button, and then lowering the zipper. I use both hands to lower my jeans past my hips where they fall to the carpet. I step out of them realizing the only thing left is the black silk thong I'm wearing.

I suddenly feel shy and I don't want that so I mask it with boldness. I take a step forward, and sink to my knees on the mattress. I crawl to him, my mouth finding his, my hand replacing his on his cock.

He lets out a deep growl, and before I can blink twice, he's ripped the thong from me with one swift pull.

"You owe me underwear, Santa Nick," I say, moving back from him.

"I want to see your pussy. On your back," he growls.

I comply, crooking one arm behind my head so that I can watch to see what he has planned. It doesn't take but a few moments before it becomes perfectly clear.

Nick moves between my legs, pulling them up and apart, slinging each one over a muscular shoulder and promptly burying his mouth at my apex, feasting on my drenched pussy with a fervor I've never known.

I can't suppress my moans of pleasure even if I wanted to, which I don't. He does this with such precision and expertise he needs to know just how fuckin' good he is at eating pussy.

Now, I've not been around all *that* much, I mean Richard was only the third guy I had ever been with, because my relationships starting in college and then after were fairly long-term for my young age and all.

I never have been one for casual sex, not that I think there is anything wrong with it, on the contrary! It's just that I seem to drift into these serious, committed relationships for whatever reason. How absolutely magical it is to have no expectations other than enjoying the moment, and the obvious skills Nick possesses, and skilled he is let me tell you!

I hear my soft-getting-louder mewling as I wriggle and writhe beneath his magic tongue and lips.

"Like that do you, Sonya?" he asks softly. "Your pussy tastes so fucking sweet."

"Nick," I whine, nearing the edge, clearly egg on my face for thinking I could outlast this man.

"What love?" he asks, his tone carrying a thread of teasing. "What do you need?"

"Uh . . . I need your cock inside me right now. I need my initial climax, and then I'm good to go for round two."

"Is that right?" he asks, a flicker of humor in his voice, as I feel his words against my heat. "Are you sure you just aren't anxious to feel my cock ring rubbing inside your cunt?"

I flush, grinding my pelvis up into his face roughly. "Well, that *too*."

Fuck! He's so good at multi-tasking that I don't even realize his hand has reached into the drawer of the hotel nightstand, and removed a condom.

Hmm?

"I want you to ride my cock," he announces, rocking back on his haunches lowering my legs so that he can roll the condom down the length of his engorged shaft. "I want to watch your beautiful face as I make you come. Are you okay with that?"

"Yes," I whimper breathlessly. "But will I feel your piercing beneath that?"

He laughs. "Greedy thing, aren't you? But yes, I'm told it doesn't inhibit the pleasure at all."

"Fuck me," I reply, nodding. "I want you to fuck him out of my mind."

He reclines back, his hands bracing my hips as he raises me up and over his torso. My hands grasp his rigid cock, and I take over, spreading my legs apart, resting my weight on my knees that are braced on either side of his hips. I lean forward a bit, raise my ass up and then sink slowly down onto his cock, my well-lubed pussy is accepting his fullness, and as I settle on to him entirely, I am pleasured by the way we fit together.

Slowly and deliberately I ride his cock up and down, using my knees to pivot me up and down, my hips swivel from side to side and yes, I feel that cock ring and it is like nothing I've ever felt before. My eyes are closed in pleasure.

His calloused hands are framing my hips; his thumbs are massaging my sides, setting the tempo of our fucking. I hear a series of soft moans escape me and I don't care. This is pure, unadulterated pleasure and I'm going to milk him dry.

"Open your eyes, Sonya," he instructs softly, his hips rising and falling in perfect rhythm. "I told you that I need to see you. Your eyes let me see everything."

I allow my eyes to flutter open and the intensity of his gaze upon me fuels the erotic moment like nothing I've ever experienced. I brush my hair back from my face, straightening my spin, rolling my hips.

"Sweet Sonya," he croons, "I want you to lean forward a bit. Yeah, like that. Let your tits brush against my chest. That's right."

And immediately it hits me as to why he wants me like this. Not only is my engorged clit rubbing against his pelvis, but the angle I'm in also provides a way for his Prince Albert piercing to massage the special spot I have deep inside, which also has become engorged.

It's almost too much for me to bear. My moans are coming quicker and louder. Our pace picks up. Marco is flexing his hips powerfully, rocking into me in such a way that I know I'm ready to come with a vengeance.

I hear his sharp intake of breath, and then he groans in manly pleasure as I cry out his name, over and over again. "Fuck me, Nick. Fuck me just like that! God don't stop," I whine, as my clitoral orgasm unwinds, and my sweet spot begins to throb for release.

He groans loudly, and then our eyes lock as we both come together, the wet release I feel from within as my pussy contracts around him again and again is involuntary, but most welcome. This has never happened to me before!

"My God," he growls, "That's it angel, keep fucking my cock just like that."

We both moan in pleasure as we keep coming together, and I know that fucking Nick is not going to be a one-time deal if I have anything to say about it.

Finally, our orgasms wind down enough that I collapse on top of him. My skin is clammy and sensitive post-orgasm. I shiver against him, and feel his strong arms wrap around me, pulling me into his warm, masculine embrace.

His lips graze the top of my head, and his hand gently brushes a couple of stray locks of hair from my face.

"Did I fuck him out of your mind, Sonya? Are you done with Richard now and done with the bad memories he left behind?"

I bite my lower lip, still feeling flushed from the most incredible sex I've ever had in my whole life. "Yes, you did. You absolutely did, Nick."

"Good. Then Santa has truly given you the most sought after gift possible this Christmas. Peace of mind, and total satisfaction of body. He no longer is the man who last possessed you. That's no small hurdle for you."

I frown in confusion, gazing over at him as he runs a hand through his tousled hair. "You mean . . . this is it. We won't be . . . umm..." My words are tangled up, but he gets it.

"Santa has so many others in need, Sonya. You don't want them to find their stockings empty this season, now do you?"

How could I possibly object to that. It would be too selfish, too damn stingy. And Nick was right. He had gotten me over the hurdle in flying colors. Nobody could take that from me. "I guess you're right. Thank you, Santa. Thank you for my best Christmas ever."

Chapter 2

DECEMBER 16TH

Libby

"Take your break now, Libby. I'll take over your register. Be back in thirty though, I have to relieve Sandy on Register twelve next.

"Got it, Vic. Thanks," I reply, grabbing my purse from underneath the counter and heading towards the exit for a well-needed smoke.

I exit through the automatic doors into the cold, misty December night air. I flick the lighter once, twice and finally on the third time I get a flame. I take a long pull from the cigarette and instantly feel the release of some tension. Filthy habit. I get that, but at twenty-one years of age, I deserve at least one vice. Smoking is mine. I get no satisfaction from anything else these days.

No sex.

No alcohol.

No man.

On the bright side? I have custody of my two nieces and one nephew that are terrific. My thirty-two year old sister passed away in a car accident last year, and her ex-husband is in prison. So I was the logical choice to take them to raise.

And because they're so damn terrific, I took a part-time cashier job at the local Big Mart so that I could make sure they had a good Christmas this year. I work full time at a toll booth from seven to three-thirty; and then from five to ten o'clock at the Big Mart.

I'm bone tired most every day, but it'll be worth it to make sure this is a good Christmas for these kids. We don't have much. A rent controlled apartment that needs all kinds of repairs, a ten year old station wagon, and bills coming out of nowhere that eventually will get paid, but we have each other.

I take another drag from my cigarette, wishing that I could simply go to my car and drive home. Soak in a bubble bath listening to some Shania Twain or Carrie Underwood, paint my toes a bright red and then crash for the night.

But I can't.

I have two more hours.

I drop my cigarette to the pavement, grinding it out with the heel of my shoe and head back inside. I've got about twenty minutes to pick up some of the stuff on the kids Christmas Wish List before I go back to my register.

I grab a cart and head toward toys. Ben, eight years old wants a remote control race car, Elizabeth, who just turned eleven wants a computer game, and Emily, the oldest at fifteen, wants a purple lava lamp. Those are just at the top of their lists. There's also the usual stuff, clothes, shoes, dolls, Nintendo games, sports jerseys, etc. But I've been doing a little bit at a time as my budget permits.

I stroll over and put a couple things in my cart and am about to start up another aisle when a display in a center aisle catches my eye.

Sensual Experience Guru Kit.

Guaranteed to put the romance back in your life.

Hah! What type of magic or voodoo is this? I look at the display and see it's a kit. Included in the kit are scented candles and oils, lubricating gel that goes from hot to cold and back when applied to the sensitive areas of the body; fancy ribbed condoms, a Barry White CD, and a book titled "The Art of Seduction: 100 Ways to Please Your Lover."

Oh for Christ sake.

$15.99 for all of that. "What a bargain," I mumble, allowing a giggle to escape. I shake my head moving my cart around the corner to the next aisle, still chuckling when BAM.

My cart collides with another. In this case, it's the store Santa's cart. He's on break as well it seems.

"Oops, so sorry," I say backing up so I can go around him, and then my eyes land on what he's got inside his cart.

Oh my God.

Sensual Experience Guru Kit.

I quickly glance back up at him, my eyes wide, and I catch the amusement in Santa's blue eyes. "No worries," he replies, "It's impossible not to collide with someone this time of year, don't you think?"

I giggle again, glancing back down into his cart. "Give my best to Mrs. Claus," I reply with a nod, and then continue past him.

"There is no Mrs. Claus."

I stop and glance back over my shoulder. I've got his full attention now. He's staring me down but not in a rude way; it's more in a curious way. He's been here since Thanksgiving, but he doesn't really socialize with anyone. I've never seen him in the break room, but then, I'm just part time and a relative newbie.

"Oh," I reply, "I just thought . . . " and I don't finish because really, what is there to say?

"Because of what's in my cart?" he asks, smiling under his fluffy white beard.

"Well . . . yeah."

"Come now, Libby. You aren't that provincial, are you?"

He knows my name? He obviously is clueless about my virginity though. But hell, I've been raising the kids since I was barely twenty, and before that, well nobody caught my interest. I was in college, and actually kind of a nerd until I was called to duty for the kids. I had to put my needs and dreams at the bottom of the priority list. That was all there was to it.

"Well, you're right on that," I sputter, "I shouldn't draw conclusions I suppose."

"I like the condoms," he says, his eyes on mine. "And I love Barry White."

I feel my face flush with his directness. "Well, good to know. I gotta get back to my register. Nice talking to you . . . Santa." I'm totally flustered at this point. A guy with a big belly, white hair and beard, has managed to totally throw me off guard with his directness. My own damn fault for making that stupid comment I guess.

I finish my shift and it's nine-thirty when I walk out to my car to start for home. Only it won't start. Dead battery.

Shit!

I pound my fists against the dashboard and fish for my cell phone to call the kids and let them know I'll be late. Elizabeth assures me everything is under control. The others are in bed and she's studying for a history exam.

"Good girl," I say, "Thanks for being you."

I end the call and dig around in my glove box for my Triple A information. Just as I'm pulling the pamphlet out, there's a soft tap on the window.

I'm startled at first, but then I see it's the store Santa. I unwind the driver side window.

"Car trouble?" he asks. "Need a ride?"

"I would gladly accept a ride, but I'll need the car in the morning for work. Battery's dead."

"Let me jump you," he offers with a grin. Damn I bet he's cute without the Santa garb I think to myself.

"Thanks, I appreciate it," I reply, popping the hood open.

Within five minutes my car sputters to life. Santa shuts the hood and comes around to my window again. "You know, Libby, you need to put a charger on that battery for a couple of hours so it'll start for you in the morning. I have a tester and charger at my place if you'd like to swing by."

I mull his offer over for a few seconds. I don't really even know this guy. For all I know, he could be some psycho Santa that gets his kicks by doing God knows what—-"

"You can follow me," he continues, "It's not far."

"Okay," I say nodding. I really have no choice at this time of night I realize. "Lead the way."

Ten minutes later I follow his shiny black pick-up truck into the parking lot of a Motel 6.

WTF?

Is he serious.

Now he's got my dander up with his presumption I'm going to put out in exchange for a charge. I'm pissed. No two ways about it. I. Am. Pissed.

I pull in next to his truck and immediately jump out to confront him. "I don't know what your game is Santa," I say abruptly, "But this isn't funny. Like at all."

He jumps down from the cab of his pick-up, a grin plastered on his face. He pulls his beard/moustache combo off and I'm immediately floored by his good looks.

Maybe not a psycho . . . but assuredly he thinks I'm a done deal for him. I can tell.

"Hey, I'm not running game on you, Libby. I live here. My tools are in the back of my truck, and if you look over there, you can see there's a power supply. That's what is needed to put your battery on the charger, okay?"

I sigh and nod. "I didn't know you lived at a motel . . . it just seemed kind of———"

"Shady?" he finishes for me. "Nothing shady about Santa, I promise. Oh, and you can call me Nick."

"Okay. Nick." I reply, wrapping my jacket tighter around me as the December winds seem to rip through me.

"Hey, here's my key card, go on up to my room if you want. I'll get your battery situated on the charger and we'll see how it goes. It's warm there and help yourself to anything I have in the fridge. It's Room 232."

I don't argue. For some reason I totally trust Nick. I take his key card, and toss him my keys. Besides that, I could really use the facilities.

His room is neat and orderly. I use the bathroom, and consider jumping in the shower to warm my chilled bones. I hesitate for about a minute and then discard my clothing, and jump under the warm jet spray of his shower. It feels so good. So relaxing, and so energizing after the day I've had. I reach for his shampoo and lather up, tilting my face up into the spray of warm water.

Ten minutes later, I step out, grabbing a fresh towel and start drying myself off. The sound of the television is coming from the room.

Oh shit.

I hope he doesn't mind my taking the liberty of using his shower. I wrap another towel around my head capturing the damp locks and hurriedly pull my clothes back on.

I step outside of the bathroom, the steam rolling out after me. I see him reclining on one of the two beds in his room. "Hope you don't mind, I couldn't resist a hot shower. It's been a long, long day."

"No problem, Lib," he says, his voice husky as he gazes over at me. "Your battery is hooked up and charging. I think I'll grab a shower too and then we can check it to see if it's making progress, how's that?"

"Fine," I reply, rubbing the towel through my hair.

He leaps off the bed and it's just then I realize he's changed into low hanging sweats that mold to his muscular frame very nicely. In three quick strides, he's in the bathroom and I hear the shower going.

I grab a comb to get the tangles out of my hair, and then relax back on the other bed.

I drift asleep for a few minutes, unaware that I've done so until I feel the weight of somebody dip onto the mattress beside me.

It's Nick. "Hey, I just checked the battery. It's halfway charged. If you need to be somewhere, it's probably good to go and will start okay in the morning. But I think you're close to needing a new one."

"Maybe I'll put that on my Christmas list," I reply. His nearness is totally getting to me. I feel my thighs clench, and that rarely happens anymore.

Maybe he can give me something I want—-something I need that he can give me. "Nick," I sigh, "I'm a virgin. I hate that at twenty-one I have to admit that, but it's the truth. I'm way out of my league here, and I'm not even sure if I'm reading the signals correctly. But . . . well, I thought I should just put it out there for you."

God I sound like a pathetic idiot.

"And what?" he replies, his eyes raking over me, "You want Santa to rid you of that pesky piece of flesh for you? Tell me, Libby. Say it."

"Yes," I answer honestly. "Just one time. Just to be done with it."

He stands up, shedding his tee and pants. "Get naked. Let's do this. Let me grab something from the closet."

I quickly shed my clothes and crawl underneath the covers, pulling the sheet up under my chin.

Nick returns momentarily placing a couple of those scented candles from the kit he'd bought today at the store. He places them on the nightstand between the two beds. I don't miss the flicker of amusement that crosses his face as he sees me covered with the sheet and blanket pulled up to my chin.

"Are you cold, Libby?" he asks with a slight smile.

"No, I'm good," I reply, trying my best to muster casualness. I don't pull it off.

He lights the candles and places one on the dresser across the room.

"These are aromatherapy," he explains. "They promote relaxation which is key to experiencing ultimate pleasure. It also provides more intimate lighting. Having sex in total darkness does not lend itself to the visual aspect of the act...watching your partner's body language and facial expressions, making words unnecessary to know what pleases each other."

I shiver a bit underneath my cocoon of covers. Santa Nick is approaching this in a very tutorial way. I like that. It makes it seem less desperate on my part.

He switches his CD player on; Barry White's deep baritone voice drifts out crooning some sexy prose. He's created some impressive ambience in his motel room.

"How much do you know about a man's body, Libby? I'm not trying to delve into your business, but it'd help me to know."

I feel my skin flush underneath all of the covers. I might as well be honest.

"Not a lot. I mean, I've lain naked with my boyfriends before. They've had their fingers on me—in me," I stuttered. "It's been a long time. I tried to give head once. The guy said I did it all wrong."

Oh God, now I am beet red from the top of my head to the tip of my toes. Nick seems fine with it.

"We won't worry about that aspect of it this tonight," he states plainly. "We're going to focus totally on your pleasure and breaking the seal, so to speak."

Nicely put.

My attention goes to Nick's face as his eyes lock with mine. He lowers his sweats, allowing the long, thick expanse of his cock to spring free. It looks to be at half-mast already.

I suck my breath in, not meaning to be quite so obvious. Christ, I'm not sure about this. It's so long and thick, and I can see he has a piercing.

I wonder how that will work with a condom. He reads my mind. "It won't be a problem. I think you'll enjoy the sensation even with a condom."

He drops a knee to the bed and pulls the covers off of me. I see his eyes peruse the length of my naked body.

He's probably seen a hundred women, and I know I have to measure up to at least some of them. I'm glad the light is by candles, it gives a soft romantic glow to everything. Maybe that kit is a bargain. It sure is coming in handy at the moment.

"Roll over onto your belly," he instructs softly.

"Really?" My voice has a slight quiver to it.

"Relax," he laughs gently. "I need to get you relaxed, baby. Trust me?"

I nod as I roll over onto my stomach. I feel Nick hover over me as he lifts a small bottle of something that he'd brought into the room with him.

I feel him pour a trail of warm, oily liquid onto my back. His hands immediately start to gently massage the warm oil into my skin. It seems to get warmer as he rubs gently in circular motions over my shoulders, between, them and then on down to my lower back.

I moan softly as he continues administering the warming oil to my hips, my butt and then on lower to the back of my thighs.

"This is a special blended massage oil," he explains softly. "It does warm upon contact to the skin. It also contains pheromones that promote a feeling of calm and relaxation. How does it feel, Libby?"

"Mmm," I sigh, "it feels so good."

Nick continues the erotic massage, covering every part of my body, including my feet which nearly cause me to climax then and there. I'd no idea that feet are considered an erogenous zone until he clues me in as he sees my reaction to his magical oil and hands.

"Roll over now. Let's do the front."

I did so without hesitation. I was eager to feel his hands with that lovely oil all over the front of me now.

It is exquisite. He takes his time, gently, soothingly rubbing all of the fear, anxiety and frustration out of me. God, this feels like heaven.

He straddles me and as his fingertips circle my nipples, I can feel his erection grow. The tip of his cock is now lightly brushing back and forth against my stomach and abdomen.

His head lowers and his tongue now circles the rosy peaks of my breasts, flicking over them, his teeth ever so gently nipping at the crests. His hands move lower, gently caressing my hips and thighs. His fingertips massage the soft folds of my pussy...plying them apart and working magic with his expert touch.

He leans back over towards the stand, wiping his hands free of the oil with a towel he'd placed there. He picks up another bottle of clear liquid.

"This is lubrication, Libby. This one's okay to be used on the genital areas. It also has a warming ingredient that'll assist in preparing you for penetration."

I watch as he pours several drops into his hand and then proceeds to massage the lubricating oil throughout the folds of my pussy, his fingers now gently entering me in soft in and out strokes. My eyes are glassy with pleasure. I want more.

"Nick," I softly moaned, "Please?"

"Not quite there yet, baby. Be patient."

He continues the gyrations with his fingers, adding a third one. While it doesn't hurt, it isn't quite as pleasurable as with just two. My hips are rotating with pleasure, moving up and down as he fingers me expertly.

"That's Santa's good girl," he coos softly to me, his voice husky and sexy. "That's just perfect."

His mouth finds mine and we kiss.

I circle my arms around his strong neck, pulling his face closer as his right hand continues fucking me with his long fingers.

I can now feel his fingers inside of me; two of them bending at the tips as if signaling a "come here" motion. Whatever spot they're tapping against inside of me feels damn good. I moan louder now.

Nick's tongue is exploring my mouth. My tongue finds his and they swirl playfully together. I love the taste of him, the scent of him, and the feel of him. God, if I wasn't ready to be fucked now, I never would be.

He leans over, not stopping what his fingers are doing below, and grabs the condom packet with his other hand.

Damn he can multi-task. He rips it open with his teeth and raises his torso up a bit.

"I want you to put this on my cock," he instructs. "Start at the tip and then just roll it on down to the base."

I nod, watching as he thrusts his hardened cock forward a bit. My fingers tremble with the pleasure that I am still feeling in my core as he continues to work his fingers in the most exquisite ways. I roll the condom down as he instructs, like I've done it a hundred times before.

His free hand checks the reservoir at the tip to make sure it hasn't been pulled down too tightly. He then grabs one of the pillows and places it under my butt to elevate it just a bit.

His mouth lowers back to mine, kissing my lips and tugging at my lower one with his teeth. His tongue finds mine again as we kiss. I can feel his fingers leaving me now to grasp the base of his erection.

I feel the head of it as his hand guides it towards me, circling the tip of it to lightly massage my clitoris. I am dripping wet for him. My hips are swiveling now, as if they have a mind of their own. Probably some primal mating instinct telling the male it's time to bring it on home.

"This is going to hurt, Libby. There's no getting around that. You need to tell me if you want me to stop, okay?"

His lips are against mine as he whispers those words to me. His warm breath sends shivers down my spine.

"I will," I whisper. "I want you now."

I feel him push himself deeper inside of me; my legs spread apart instinctively to welcome him in. My hips continue to gyrate against him as he gives a quick thrust to bury himself a bit deeper.

Shit. It fucking hurts.

His mouth continues to devour mine, his teeth nipping at my lips, trying to take my mind off of "ground zero," I suppose. I continue kissing him back and moving beneath him. My fingers are splayed across his back, my nails tracing circular patterns as my hips move in unison with them. I promise myself I will not cry out.

He gives one final thrust that causes him to moan, as if in pain. It is nothing compared to the searing white pain that shoots through me and the scream from me that follows.

He stills himself inside of me. "Are you okay?"

A single tear rolls down my cheek, but I nod being the "trooper" I am. "The worst is over, right?" I ask between clenched teeth.

"I think so, baby. I need to move inside of you, though. Can you hang with it?"

"I can," I murmur, unconvinced. I asked for this, and by God, Nick was delivering.

And then he moves and it's less painful. He does so again and again. He murmurs things to me; dirty sexy things which I find quite arousing, and kissing my mouth passionately as he does so.

"You're so fucking sweet," he whispers against my lips. "God, you're so sweet and beautiful."

His rhythm increases bit by bit. Each time, he changes tempo he asks if I'm okay. I am. I'm more than okay.

My legs are now wrapped tightly around his hips. My freshly-massaged feet and toes are digging into his muscular ass with a vengeance. This no longer hurts. This feels *damn* fine, as a matter of fact.

I feel a different sensation now as Nick continues to rock in and out of me. His hands pull my hips up at an angle so that his cock is hitting that same 'come hither' spot that his fingers tapped earlier.

Now it's different. He swiveled his hips so that the tip is circling it over and over again. He changes course and rocks into me so it hits full force in the center of that seemingly engorged bundle of nerve endings.

Damn!

I feel warmth spreading throughout my core that seems to be building up into a vortex of pure pleasure...begging for release.

I hear Nick groan and I'm right there with him.

"Oh my God," I yell. "Oh God, don't stop!"

I can't believe it's me shouting those things to him, like some back alley whore, but I don't care.

Nick rocks in and out of me; both of us moaning and saying things, dirty things to each other. Words that I've never used before spew from my lips as the release of my climax unravels magically and fluidly from me.

We come together and it rocks big time.

I have never, ever felt anything so primal and yet so pleasurable in my entire life. I feel as if our bodies, for that moment in time, were fused together as one.

I now knew what all of the fuss was about... It all makes perfect sense to me.

As the waves of pleasure wash over us both, I can feel my toes curled up against Nick's back.

Our climax starts to wind down, leaving me with a delightful tingling sensation from head to toe. I place my hands on either side of this man's beautiful face and place t kisses all over it.

His fingers are tangled in my hair as his arm had somehow ended up curled above my head on the pillow. His tongue traces over my lips as he whispers softly to me. "Merry Christmas, Libby. Santa thinks you've been a very good girl this year."

It takes me a few moments to catch my breath and collect my thoughts. "I'm glad my car wouldn't start tonight, Santa. You've made this the best holiday ever."

"Santa is always happy to stuff a stocking or two," he says, pulling out of me and checking below for the damage. "And thank you Libby for trusting me to be the first. It's been an honor. How about we toast to having our batteries charged?"

"I'll drink to that," I reply with a giggle. "You're welcome to stuff my stocking any time."

And he pours us each an eggnog with a shot of rum and we indeed toast one another.

I got home after midnight and checked the kids. All safe and sound in their beds, visions of sugar plums dancing in their heads.

Christmas would never be a bummer again.

Chapter 3

Stacy and Lacey

"Well I don't have to tell you two ladies you are both just perfect to play Santa's helper elves! Identical twins, how lucky can I get, right?"

The two blond haired, blue eyed twins look at one another and giggle. "I can't believe we're doing this, Lace," Stacy says to her twin. "I hope nobody from the university recognizes us!'

"Oh who cares," Lacey replies, "It's a hundred bucks a day for the next five days . . . umm... we do start today right, Ms. Lancaster?"

The gray haired woman behind the desk peruses their applications one last time and nods. "Be back here at noon for your fitting, you'll clock in then and one of you will start in Lay Away pulling orders, the other helps Santa. At five o'clock, whomever is working Lay Away comes back up to help Santa. It gets really busy then. You can alternate your lunch break so Santa always has a helper. Any questions?"

"What exactly do we help Santa with?" Stacy asks.

"Getting the kids on and off his lap, giving out candy, taking photos, and listening to the little brats stutter out their wish list. Usual holiday crap."

Lacey gives Stacy a sidelong glance. Obviously Ms. Lancaster was a Scrooge when it came to the whole Christmas holiday traditions. "We can handle it no problem, Ms. Lancaster," Stacy chirps enthusiastically. "We love kids."

"Lovely," she replies, handing them each a time card, "See you back here at noon. Good luck, Ladies."

∞

"How's it going?" Lacey asks approaching the Santa Land display where her twin had just snapped a picture of a toddler girl crying the whole time she sat on Santa's lap.

"Hell, Lace, is it almost time to clock out? This shit is grueling. Now I understand why Lancaster has the attitude she has."

Lacey chuckles, "What about all that stuff about us loving kids? We already had the jobs."

"The only fringe benefit I can see in this gig is maybe doing Santa," Stacy replies.

Her twin grows suddenly silent. The mood has taken a turn, and Stacy quickly puts her arm around Lacey. "Hey Lace, I'm sorry. I know I just touched on a sore subject with you, but honestly? You need to get on with life and not let what happened ruin your chances for a happy and sexy future, you know? I didn't mean to make you feel bad."

"I know you didn't. And it's easy for you to say that to me, but it didn't happen to you. You can't know how damaged and self-conscious I feel. No guy would find me sexy the way I look ... now. Jason didn't stick around very long now did he?"

Stacy hugs her sister warmly, and murmurs comfortingly, "Jason is a dick head. Fuck him."

The somber moment shared between the sisters doesn't go unnoticed by Nick, and he wonders what could have possibly happened to Lacey to make her feel self-conscious and damaged. She looks positively perfect to Nick. He makes it his mission to dig deeper. He needs to see how he can spread some holiday cheer to Lacey. Perhaps there was a need he could fill with Lacey.

At the end of the shift, he thanks both of the twin elves for their help, and asks Stacy if she might stay a couple of minutes to help him get some more stockings stuffed before their next shift the following day. "No probs," she replies a bit flirtatiously. "See you back at the dorm, Lacey."

As soon as they begin working, Nick takes the opportunity to let Stacy know he couldn't help but overhear their exchange. "I'm not trying to pry, Stacy, but I can't help but he curious as to what makes Lacey think she's damaged. She's every bit as beautiful and sexy as you."

Stacy stops sorting through the candy on the table. "I shouldn't say anything to anyone—-she's do damn sensitive about it even though what happened wasn't her fault. She was the victim, and the worst part is, her ex-boyfriend cause the accident, but he walked away without a scratch. He ruined her life!"

"Please," Nick persists, "I'd like to help if I can. You can tell me, I promise it won't go any further."

"Well, since you do seem like a real Santa, I guess there's no problem in telling you. But I doubt if there's anything you can do, but it's really nice that you want to. Okay, so Lacey was in a car accident with her boyfriend at the time, Jason. The accident was his fault, he'd been drinking, but he didn't want to stick around and wait for the police to get there. He didn't want another DUI on his record."

"Go on," Nick prods, "Was she hurt?"

"That's putting it mildly," Stacy replies with a frown. "Her ankle was shattered. Jason wouldn't take her to the hospital because he didn't want her to have to explain how it happened. He told her to keep it propped, and to keep ice on it. Long story short, it turned gangrene. She had to have her left leg amputated to just below the knee. She wears a prosthesis."

"Oh, I see. And that is the reason she feels she's damaged and not beautiful?"

"Well, duh! I mean Jason the asshole dropped her like a used condom, and he caused it all. He told her he just couldn't bear to look at her stump. I mean, I try to encourage her to stay positive, but in all honesty, can you expect guys to overlook something like that?"

"I would," Nick replies matter-of-factly. "A woman is so much more than their legs, or their breasts or their asses. She has beautiful eyes, and her lips are full and sensual—-she has a great heart too, I can tell."

There's a moment of silence between the two as Stacy reflects on Santa's words. "Well, we are *twins,* ya know? Don't I have those things too?"

Nick chuckles. "Definitely the eyes and lips. Not so sure about the heart though, Stacy."

She looks injured.

Nick certainly didn't want to insult her, but as near as he could tell, Stacy didn't lack for male attention. He had seen it all afternoon when she'd been working with him. The smallest of breaks in the stream of kids and she was on her phone, texting, taking selfies, and reading return texts. "How long has your sister gone without?" he asks bluntly.

The question startles Stacy momentarily.

"You mean . . . without sex?"

"Well, duh," Nick teases, "What did you think I was talking about . . . chocolate?"

Stacy giggles, her mood once again playful. "Not since Jason. So, it's been like a year and a half I guess. Why do you want to know? Got a dildo for her stocking? Let me save you the gesture. She has plenty."

Nick grabs his notebook, and scribbles down his address at the Motel 6. "This is where I stay. There's an all night diner right next to it. Have her there around 9:30 this evening. Drop her off in front. Tell her you're going to find a place to park and then leave. I'll make sure she gets back to campus after I rock her world."

"What?" she gasps, "Why should I trust you?"

"Because. I'm Santa remember? And Stacy—this is our secret. I don't want Lacy to think I'm going to pity fuck her because I assure you, that isn't the case."

Lacey

If this doesn't turn out well, I just may commit sistercide. This is only one of the many things swimming through my mind as I freshen up in the bathroom of Room 232 of the Motel 6. I sit on the commode, and remove my prosthesis. I inspect my leg—or what's left of it I should say. There's nothing really gross about it anymore. It simply is a healed stump. No redness, no puckered skin . . . it's smooth and tapered. But it lacks a calve, ankle and foot. The prosthesis is a good one. I can walk normally, even jog which I do to keep the rest of the muscles on that leg good and strong. My doctor says I've done amazingly well.

But now? Well now is time to see just how turned off this guy is gonna be when he sees me.

Let me back track to about an hour ago.

What the hell was with Stacy dropping me off, and telling me that somebody inside was waiting for me and then driving off like a bat out of hell? At first I thought it was a bad joke until I saw the guy come to the door of the diner and smile as he opened the door for me.

It was freezing out. What choice did I have. I palmed the phone in my coat pocket, feeling some sense of security knowing it was there. Besides, this was a public diner. There were probably twenty other people inside. What harm could come to me inside where at least it was warm?

I step inside as he holds the door for me, and motions me to the first booth that lines the windowed wall. "Please have a seat. I've ordered one of your favorites, apple crumb pie with warm caramel sauce and a coffee, no sugar just cream."

"How . . . how did you know that?" I ask, as I slide into the booth and he takes a seat across from me.

"A little elf told me," he says with a chuckle. "Hi, my name is Nick. I saw you working today at Big Mart. I had to meet you. Hope you don't think this is creepy?"

Oh no. Not at all.

"Umm . . . it was probably my sister you met. Her favorite dessert is the same as mine. She seems to have played a joke on the both of us." This guy is so stunningly handsome, I can barely take my eyes off of him. Dark brown wavy hair, a dimpled chin, and a lopsided grin revealing straight white teeth. True hunk. No lie.

"Is your sister's name Lacey?" he asks.

"No . . . that's my name."

"Then I have the right girl," he replies, reaching across the table and placing his hand on mine. "I wanted to have coffee with you. I wasn't sure how to ask. Your sister helped. Don't be mad at her."

This was all too confusing; my thoughts confettied trying to figure out when Stacy had been given the opportunity to do some stud shopping for me. But really, should I look a gift horse in the mouth? Our mother had always preached that to us, and to this day, it still confuses me but it seems to fit the current situation so I'll go with it.

"I'm confused is all. What exactly is it you expect from me?"

"I expect nothing. What I hope is that we'll have dessert and coffee, talk a bit, and then if you feel like it, go over to my place at the motel. I'd like to make love to you."

My eyes widen with his blunt revelation.

"You know, don't you?"

"What I know is that you have beautiful eyes, and your lips tempt me beyond reason. I also suspect that inside, you're every bit as beautiful as you are on the outside. You're not a pretty package that's empty inside, like the ones they put under the Christmas tree at Big Mart. No way. You are overflowing with the goods, Lacey. I just want in. Just once."

And how the hell could I deny him—-deny myself what I truly needed? Proof that no matter what happened to my body, and regardless of the small part of me that's missing, I'm still a sexual being, fully capable of giving and enjoying pleasure.

I clear my throat, my pulse quickens. Not only will this be a first in almost two years, but it will be my first ever for a random hook-up? How cool was that I thought. And then I heard myself speak words that I felt comfortable saying. "I'd like that Nick," I reply just as our server places our coffee and desserts in front of us. "I think I'd like that very much."

I shrug on the guest robe that is hanging neatly on the back of the door, take a deep breath, and hobble out of the bathroom, to the inviting bed he's turned down for the both of us.

We sit facing each other on the bed. His hands gently reach over, cupping my chin and pulling my face towards his. "You look beautiful, Lacey," he says huskily. "You have everything that's important to a man. To this man."

We kiss, gently at first, and then allow the passion to slowly mount. Our tongues explore each other as lovers do for the first time. It's all unexplored territory for the both of us. I love this part.

His fingers softly caress one of my breasts, his thumb circling the nipple and bringing it to a peak, then moving to the other. My hands are now on his back, rubbing his muscles, his beautiful skin, loving the feel of him against me.

He pushes me back so that his lips and tongue can capture my breasts, one at a time. He takes his time with each, his tongue circling each nipple, and his teeth nip gently at the nubs making my skin tingle with pleasure and anticipation. This feels so damn good. I moan softly.

"I want to be inside of you, Lacey. I *need* to be inside of you" he breathes huskily.

I raise myself up and he lowers my panties. I scoot off of him, so that he can remove his boxers.

His erection springs free. And like the wanton hussy I am at the moment, I don't hesitate before wrapping my fingers around it, lowering my lips to taste it.

This is familiar to me. My tongue runs the length of it up and down, back and forth, and then swirls around the swollen head. My tongue feels his cock ring which I glimpsed as soon as he'd removed his boxers. I love the feel and the taste of him, because he for this moment in time, he is giving himself to me as if he were my lover, not just a random guy getting laid. He chose me. That makes all the difference in the universe to me.

I hear his sharp intake of breath as my teeth gently graze the sensitive tip. At the same time, I feel his fingers as he gently plys the sensitive folds of my sex, bringing me waves of pleasure with his touch. I feel him insert a finger and then another. I am immediately wet for him. I moan again softly as his fingers hit my special place.

"I know, Lacey," he soothes. "I want it, too." He pulls his hand from me and quickly grabs a condom from the drawer of his nightstand, sheathing himself.

He lifts me up, and places me over his erection. Our eyes lock as he lowers me down onto him until he fills me completely. We are facing each other, my legs parted on either side of his hips.

I hear his soft, husky moans and I feel my muscles flexing, squeezing him instinctively. His hands are on my hips, moving me up and down the length of him. My hands are on his shoulders, my fingernails digging into his skin with the intensity of the pleasure.

I ride him as he continues to thrust up inside of me, harder now. My fingernails dig deeper as I reach the peak and begin the sweet descent into my orgasm. And he is right there with me, chanting my name like a prayer, as his lips capture mine with frenzied passion and carnal need.

We climax as one, our primal moans mixed together as we ride it out, one pleasurable release after another.

Afterwards, he gently lifts me off of him, and I shift to the side and curl up next to him. Our skin is damp and sticky. I trace his delicious treasure trail with my fingers while his arms encircle me protectively. He kisses the top of my head over and over again. "You are amazing, Lacey. Simply amazing. I can't imagine any man not wanting you. Thank you for this."

"No," I whisper against his chest. "Thank you, Nick. This is the best Christmas I've had in a long, long time."

I come awake in Nick's bed. We dozed off, or at least I must've but I'm wide awake now as I feel his tongue delivering the most delicious pleasure I've ever felt to my pussy.

"Hey you. I'm not ready to call it a night yet. How about a little wake-me-up?" he asks, his lips now on mine. I can taste myself on his mouth. Salty sweet.

"I'm game, Nick. Don't stop," I whisper against his lips. I feel his smile.

He lowers his mouth back to my belly; and his tongue circles my naval, and then burns a hot trail south. My hands have found their place in his mass of thick, dark hair. My fingers tangle in his locks as soft whimpers escape my lips.

His tongue once again finds my wetness, and I feel each stroke as he laps up my juices as if some sweet nectar. "Fuck, you taste so good," he murmurs huskily. "You've got one sweet pussy, Lacey."

Nick continues French kissing my sex, as my hips instinctively roll against him, wanting him deeper. He obliges my unspoken desire, his tongue plunging inside of me, and his fingers right there beside it.

"Oh God," I cry out. "Bloody hell!"

And I come in his mouth and on his fingers. With each pulsating release of my orgasm, he is right there sucking my pussy, drinking it in, and moaning his own pleasure, which makes it even hotter. My hands are gripping the sheets, as my climax rocks through every muscle and nerve ending in my body, rendering me totally mindless other than moaning his name over and over again.

As it ebbs, I feel my heart rate start to slow a bit, and I can finally catch my breath. My hand releases the bottom sheet and I feel my muscles relax.

"Holy hell," I rasp, "I'm sorry I came so fast," I apologize. "I wanted to wait until you were..."

He rests back on his haunches and gives me a sexy, lazy grin, "Inside of you," he finishes.

"Well, yeah."

"Don't worry, Lacey. The night is young. I have all the time you're willing to give me."

"Game on, Nick," I whisper, scooting myself lower so that my face is even with his cock. "My turn."

As a side note to the readers, you'll be happy to know that after the hot, steamy, sexy night spent with Santa Nick, Lacey was no longer afraid to cultivate relationships with men. She learned that she was more than her imperfection, and any man worthy of her, be it a relationship or a hook-up needed to be more than their imperfections as well. She never knew that "Nick" was the Big Mart Santa, and Stacy kept to her word that she would never tell!

Chapter 4

DECEMBER 22ND.

Brandon

Here it is.

Three fucking days before Christmas and I've never been lonelier. It's my own fault. I'm the King of Deception it seems. I deserve to be alone.

I'm twenty-two years old. There's no excuse for this. I've known I was gay since I was twelve. What the hell have I been thinking? I know damn well what I've been thinking. Probably the same thing so many other dudes have thought when trying to fight the truth about their sexuality.

Pussy—-lot's of it. It is the cure for homosexuality.

Wrong!

So. Damn. Wrong.

And not just wrong for me, but wrong for the chicks I've used in trying like hell to make that fallacy come true.

The latest victim?

Brittany. My fiancé for the past two years.

I just couldn't live the lie anymore. I had to tell her. She freaked - could I really blame her?

Hell no.

Of course, she did go off the deep end just a bit. Recoiling from me; pulling her legs up underneath her chin and rocking back and forth in the near-fetal position, and chanting shit about having AIDS because of my lying ass.

I told her over and over again that I'd never been with a dude—-which is the honest to God truth, but she wasn't buying it. She scheduled a blood test over the phone while I was still at her apartment, and then told me to get my queer ass out of her home, and out of her life.

I was good to go with that.

I left feeling miserable, more for the fact that I'd been totally honest with her when I said I'd never played out my natural sexual preference. Somehow I thought it would sound noble. It sounded like a lie to her, and to me it was just downright pathetic.

I came from a staunch Catholic family. I grew up being taught sex before marriage was a sin, and I could only imagine that sex with the same gender was unforgiveable. In all honesty though, my parents were loving and forgiving to me for all of my mistakes growing up. I just never wanted to test them on this issue though.

I enter Wal-Mart, to do some last minute Christmas shopping for the folks. And maybe for myself. I'm an only child and there are expectations, I get that. But yeah, my guilt is obviously showing through because I know I've already bought way too many Christmas gifts for the folks. I have to break the news to them of my broken engagement smack dab on Christmas Day. It isn't going to be pleasant, I know that, because what will follow is my outing myself. I can't hide from the truth any longer, and I won't live a lie for my parents' sake—-or my soul's sake if they are hell bent on believing that crap.

SANTA'S STOCKING STUFFERS

I wade through aisle after aisle overflowing with the most frantic of humanity doing their holiday shopping. I toss a few stocking stuffer into my cart, some DVD's that I know Mom and Pop will love, along with some scented candles they always have burning in their bathrooms and then head over to the book aisle.

I'm skimming through the "Self-Help" categories, and no—thank you very much—I don't need to know how to stay on a budget, or how to get rich by using coupons, or even how to get my dog to stop licking his balls. Yeah, the last one is totally made-up. I'm just about ready to give up when I spot a title that hits home big time.

Coming Out Later In Life.

I get that being twenty-two may not qualify as being *late in life*, but in sexual awakening terms? It totally fits.

I grab the paperback edition, knowing full well I will check this out in ebook form once I get home, but first I want to satisfy my curiosity to see if it looks to be a valid read.

As I stand there, leafing through the chapters, I fail to notice that my cart is rolling away from me until I hear it crash against the display at the end of the aisle, and a pyramid of the Latest CD Christmas Releases tumble to the floor with a loud echo of distress.

Shit.

I hurriedly scramble to the scene just as the Big Mart Santa is approaching from across the aisle to assist.

We collide.

The paperback I'm still holding, falls at his feet with a resounding thud.

Oh God. Now I'll have Santa judging me.

Great.

Just freakin' great.

"Let me help," he says, gathering up a handful of CD's, acting like he hasn't read the title of the book I dropped at his feet.

We restock the display until some associates arrive and finish the job.

"Thanks, Santa," I say, holding my hand out to him.

He gives my hand a hearty shake. "Here is something for you....?"

"Brandon," I reply, somehow knowing he wants my name.

"Here is something for you, Brandon," he continues, reaching into his pocket for a small stocking with a candy cane sticking out of it.

"Uh . . . no, it's fine," I reply, "I really don't do sweets. Bad for the teeth, you know?"

"I think there might be something more interesting if you look," he replies with a wink.

I take it from him, not quite understanding his message, until later. Once in my car, I empty the contents of the stocking. There's piece of paper folded up. When I open it, I'm surprised at what it says:

Come see me. Room 232 at Motel 6 off of Branson Road after ten P.M. I think Santa has what you need.

Is this a joke?

The note doesn't look pre-printed at all. What are the chances Santa gives out a handful of these every day?

Or is it possible a Big Mart Santa understands my dilemma? Am I that easy to read? I need to think about this,

Long and hard. But not for too long. This could very well be the coming out opportunity of a lifetime.

I go home, shower and change. I grab a bite to eat, wrap a few more presents, and feed the dog.

There's no putting off the inevitable. I'm going to the Motel 6. I convince myself it's out of curiosity more than anything else. And if the dude turns out to be a psycho, I can handle myself. I'm no wimp in case I haven't mentioned it. I'm 6 foot 2, one hundred ninety-five pounds and I work out like a fiend. No shame there at all.

I lock the door of my apartment and head out to the Motel 6 and what I hope turns out to be dipping my first toe—-or dick if you will—into my true sexuality.

Nick

I realize it's a long shot that Brandon will show tonight, but it was worth a try nonetheless. It didn't take the book he was perusing to fall at my feet to know the guy had an internal battle going on with his sexual identity. And by my estimation of his age, it was taking him far too long to shed his denial. I can help him, and I want to do just that. I'm bisexual which makes my seasonal giving all that much more versatile. So far this season, I've given the gift of seduction and sexual fulfillment to a myriad of those in need. I hope Brandon turns out to be another.

My dick twitches at the notion of being his first. Of showing him how it's done for the ultimate of pleasure. My instincts tell me he'll be a bottom, which makes him even more tantalizing as I enjoy topping when given the choice.

I don't want to get ahead of myself though, so I busy myself in prepping the room for his potential arrival.

Musk oil in the scented wall plug-ins to promote testosterone rushes. Changing the bed linens to my own black set I brought from my *real* home. Have to play the masculinity card, right? Plenty of scotch and Irish whiskey in my portable wet bar, also brought from home. My supply of condoms and lube were all good. I selected some music for our tete a tete. Some Creed and of course, ZZ Top. Great for the rhythm.

I shower and then I wait. It's almost ten. My adrenaline pulses through my veins at the thought of another deflowering this holiday season. One of each. How miraculous is that?

A few minutes after ten, I hear a tentative knock on the door. When I open it I see him there. He's dressed in jeans and a hoodie. Totally in his early twenties I decide, stepping aside to allow him to enter my room. "Welcome, Brandon," I greet. "I'm so glad you decided to stop by this evening."

We've had a couple of cocktails over the past thirty minutes. Santa decides it's about time for shit to get real. Brandon is relaxed. He is feeling the groove, I can read the signs in his body language and the fact he's talking more—-a lot more.

"Come here," I tell him softly yet sternly. He obliges, his steps sure if not a little slow. "Don't be hesitant."

My eyes rake his body one more time, the physical perfection of it an alluring beacon. Tall, wholesome and breathtakingly handsome was a catch-phrase invented for the sole purpose of describing this man.

"I'm not hesitant," he tells me but I'm not sure who he's trying to convince; me or himself.

"It's okay to be nervous, it's your first time. But lucky for you, I'm going to let you do the fucking. I'm pretty sure you know how to do that. Let's get naked."

We both chuckle, as we start undressing. Brandon's eyes never waver from my gaze, like he's trying to figure something out. "Yeah," he replies, "I was engaged for a couple of years. Couldn't go through with it. It was a total lie."

"You did the right thing, Brandon," I say as I drop my boxers, stepping out of them and take the remaining step towards him. I close the distance between us, our bodies not fully touching but our combined heat cocooning us, creating our own bubble of lust. "I'm going to touch you, Brandon. Then, I want your hands to explore me. My erogenous zones are different than a woman's; find them and take advantage of that knowledge," I instruct him as I place a tentative hand on his pectoral, pinching lightly at his erect nipple.

His sharp inhale tells me two things—I hurt him and he likes it. So, I do it again. This time he's expecting it, and I feel his cock bob as it bumps against mine.

With one last step, I bring our cocks together, a soft caress of hot flesh and burning need. "Do you feel that?" I ask him in a low murmur and wrap my hands around our embracing shafts, their combined girths too thick for just one hand.

I rub and stroke us slowly, at first, speeding up my movements; our gazes never faltering. As I masturbate us, Brandon lifts his hands with a confidence he didn't possess mere minutes before and brings them to my shoulders.

The feverish touch spreads across my flesh with pinpricks of anticipation. His exploring hands slide down the length of my arms, stopping when they reach mine, and he begins thrusting his hips as he joins me in our ministrations. With shaky breaths, our movements become faster, more confident, the strokes longer as our bodies inch closer to the source of pleasure.

Bringing my mouth to Brandon's jaw, I let my tongue run along his stubble, reveling in the feel of rough masculinity.

As our lips meet, I glide against them, back and forth lightly; the air between them mixing into its own fragrance of desire. "Open up for me, Brandon."

I don't know where the words come from. They are too intimate, too loving. I need to keep my mind on sex and set aside the niggling warmth growing exponentially within my chest.

"Believe me, Nick, I have never been this open before."

Fuck.

My tongue is suddenly invading his open mouth, the action spurred on by the earnest show of vulnerability. We tango to the sound of our beating hearts, our ragged breaths, the rubbing of our sweat-coated skin. I feel as though I'm inhaling him straight into my lungs, tasting his every nuance, feeling his every emotion. It's heady; it's fucking alluring like a super drug that suddenly makes everything clear and simple.

Releasing our throbbing cocks, I raise my hands to his jaw, clenching my fingers into the flesh behind his ears and attempt to thrust my tongue even further into his mouth. I want to sink deep inside him on a level that obliterates the purely sexual and enters a realm I didn't even know existed for men like myself.

Brandon mirrors my stance, our bodies touching on every inch right down to our feet aligned side by side.

Pulling myself away, panting like a sixteen-year-old getting his first taste of pussy or cock...whatever, I lose what little control I thought I was holding.

"On the bed, Brandon," I say through clenched teeth, desperately trying to remember this is his first time. I'm going to let him top for his first time. It will help his stamina and self-confidence. "I need you inside me, right now."

Brandon's eyes are glazed over, his mouth swollen from our mutual assaults, his skin a pink hue of lust unmasking all his well-hidden emotions. He wants this as much I do, and it's time to get to it.

Looking over on the night stand, I locate the lube. and reach for it. Scooting back up to the center of the bed, I open the tube and squirt the lube onto my palm and begin spreading it along my aching dick before reaching my balls. I'm lying on my back, my legs wide open, giving him the perfect view for what I intend to do.

Watching Brandon drinking in the reality of a man spread open for him is turning me on. I'm that man. Not some two-bit escort slut. Not some gigolo getting paid to give Brandon carnal pleasures for the first time. Me.

Santa Fucking Claus.

My hand cups my balls, rolling them slowly between my fingers while my pinky gently applies the lotion on my perineum, dangerously close to my puckered hole. Brandon's eyes are ablaze, dilated with a force of nature that I cannot wait to unleash for him.

"Touch me, Brandon. You need to know who you're fucking. I don't want you to pretend your dick will be inside some random woman. Come over here and touch me, know who I am. Put your hand on my cock, your fingers inside my ass and make me come. Preferably in your mouth."

Brandon approaches me, one foot in front of the other, as he runs his fisted hand up from the root of his proud cock to the tip of his cum-beading head, spreading the delicious liquid around.

I lick my lips, my body remembering the taste of him.

Handing him the tube of lube, I open my legs further to accommodate him as he kneels between my thighs. The look on his face exudes animalistic desire, a want borne only from the deep driving need to fuck.

Flipping open the tube, he holds it up, just above me, and lets the contents run down my exposed balls, sliding perfectly on my expectant hole and down the rest of my spread crack. This man who merely an hour earlier was hesitant in his moves now owns his every action.

I shiver as I feel his questioning fingers rubbing the lube over my cock, my balls and finally around my entrance. Brandon's eyes dart up to mine, looking completely enthralled, like he's discovered the hidden treasures of Atlantis. I like that look because I put it there.

Slowly, I feel the pressure of his finger pushing inside, careful not to hurt me.

"It's so wrong and yet...it feels so fucking good," he says softly as his finger enters me easily with the help of the lube.

I can't help myself. I palm my dick and begin stroking myself to the rhythm of his finger fucking. It's good but it's not enough, I need more.

"Don't be shy, Brandon," I say. "It's only you and me. Put in another finger. Stretch me out and fucking put your dick inside me."

Maybe that was a bit forceful but my patience is about to strangle me if he doesn't accelerate this. Brandon's eyes snap up to me, the innocence in his eyes gone, the animal back with a force that almost has me fearing for my ass.

Literally.

I feel the pressure of a second finger and their scissoring motion before he continues, "Hold on, because I'm about to pummel you, and for the first time in my life, I'll know exactly what I'm doing."

Shit...

Leaning away from me, Brandon slides his hand over to the night stand and grabs a condom.

With quick, practiced movements, this god-like man above me sheathes his cock and is about to plunge inside me, but something stops him.

I almost howl with frustration, the anticipation digging its claws into my libido. But then his head bends over my painful erection and as he darts his tongue out, I feel the wet heat sliding up the underside of my shaft. I swear to fucking God I just about come right there on the spot. I replace my finger where his had been, keeping myself ready for him while my other hand runs through my hair, my back arching, reaching for more.

Brandon's eyes are closed until he reaches the bulbous head and my cum coats his lips. They snap open, staring directly at me and with deliberate moves, he licks his teeth, coating them with my essence before dropping down and savagely attacking my mouth with desperation, his palms flat on the bed on either side of my face.

The taste of my pre-cum spurring my need, I sink my hands into his hair, my fingers digging into his scalp, nails scraping against flesh. My hips rock upward bumping into his cock, my body begging for more.

I pull slightly away and whisper, "Please, Brandon. Just put your dick inside me before I lose my fucking mind."

That's when I feel it. The head of his cock is resting against my asshole, as his entire sweat-streaked body covers mine, our mouths fusing into one.

We both grunt as he pushes inside me slowly, the vibrations swallowed within our kiss. The pinch of pain accompanies the overwhelming pleasure, his thickness enveloped by my hot walls trapping him. Inch by torturous inch, he finds his way until his balls slap against my ass. He's completely buried to the hilt as we both still and stare at each other.

Right before my eyes, I see a man who has been hiding his natural tendencies, but with one thrusting motion has just realized that he's home. That's right, I did this. I'm responsible for his revelation.

"I'm pretty sure you know what to do at this point," I tell him through clenched teeth, wanting him to thrust, needing him to pummel my prostate so I can come like a fucking volcano.

"Oh yeah, I know exactly what I'm doing. Just a head's up...hold on for dear life, I'm going to fucking ruin you."

And that's exactly what Brandon does.

Pulling out slowly, he thrusts back in hard enough to have my body sliding across the bed. Grunts from us both are like an erotic melody that only turns us both into raging beasts. Still bracing himself on the mattress, my hands anchored in his silky dark hair, Brandon's dick rhythmically thrusts into me.

Owning me.

Claiming me for a time.

Little does he know I'm leading this dance no matter how hard he fucks me. "Fuck...yeah," I groan as his thrusts get more intense, more frantic, and more needy.

"I'm gonna come, Nick. I'm going to fucking come so hard," he grunts.

"Do it, let me milk you dry," I answer as one hand drops down to my cock, pumping it so as to time our orgasms perfectly.

"God, yes...fuck...I'm..."

We both freeze, Brandon's spine arches, his head falling back with eyes tightly closed, his mouth in a grimace of utter ecstasy. He is magnificent, he is a god, and he is fucking everything.

With that image forever tattooed into my mind, my hips spasm as my own cum spurts from the head of my cock and lands directly on his glistening chest, already wet from the exertion.

Brandon collapses on top of me, my cum coating our bodies, mixing with our sweat.

"Holy hell," he growls. "To think of what I've been missing all this time . . . "

I run a hand over his chest. "My turn next, Brandon."

∞

Brandon

This has been the greatest experience of my life. Nick has shown me in just one hour what I've been depriving myself since puberty. I can't believe the intensity of it, the pure satisfaction I reached for the first time ever. How could I have cheated myself of the ultimate sexual pleasure that I crave? That my body is made for?

We clean up and relax with another cocktail, though I don't need one. My nerves are fine, my body simply craves more fulfillment. I want to feel him inside of me now. I need to have completion of my sexuality that I know he can provide.

"Are you ready?" Nick asks, as if he magically can read my mind.

Am I ready? I have no fucking clue what is happening, but I do know one thing. My body is craving every touch of this man.

I nod. "Absolutely."

Nick pushes my thighs further apart then places his hands on the backs of my knees and pulls my legs over his shoulders forcing my body to sink into the bed, my ass in plain view.

Suddenly, I'm wondering if I look enticing. I trim my nether regions, but shit, I've never looked at my asshole thinking anyone would have a front and center view of it. My thoughts are all over the fucking place when I feel the hot, wet firmness of Nick's tongue swiping down my ass crack.

My entire body shudders under the incredible sensation, my every nerve ending lighting up like a fucking Christmas tree. My entire blood supply rushes to my dick. My synapses concentrate on one singular thing, my ass clenching for more.

"Relax, Brandon, and enjoy it all. I promise, it's all good." Nick's voice is like honey dripping straight from the bee hive—raw and silky, making my every muscle melt into nothingness.

"That's it, Brandon," he says before his tongue swipes again, forcing goose bumps across every inch of my skin.

The thought doesn't have time to register that I feel the same wetness prodding my hole, licking to entice my opening then slowly making its way inside. Closing my eyes, I try to imagine what he's doing in my mind and, to my surprise, instead of feeling horror I feel pure, unadulterated lust consume me completely.

"Holy shiiiit..." I breathe out because I have never in my twenty-some years ever felt anything better than this. Not with pussy. Not from a woman's tongue even.

Instinctively, I sink down further and spread wider inviting Nick deeper, taking more, pushing me farther into oblivion. My hands suddenly shoot out to my lover's head and grip onto his hair for dear life, my hips thrusting, silently begging for more.

"Yes, fuck, yes..." I chant over and over again as Nick's mouth completely takes over and his tongue buries inside me, stretching me for what I know is a preamble to what is happening next.

Pulling back, Nick licks his way up and suddenly engulfs my cock inside his talented mouth almost gagging at my girth.

As I'm fucking Nick's face from below him, I feel a digit penetrate me. Although I tense at first, I can't help but enjoy it, with his lips sucking my cock; my emotions are all over the place.

And then something happens.

Nick's finger curls into what feels like a come-hither motion and my entire body jumps from the couch, my cock disappearing completely into my lover's mouth and before I know what the fuck is going on, I'm coming down his throat like a fucking teenage virgin getting his first blowjob.

"What ...was that?" I'm panting, and my breathing is a complete erratic mess, my skin burning from the best damn orgasm I have ever experienced.

"That, baby...was your prostate. Welcome to my world, Brandon," he says licking his lips like a singer who's here especially to seduce me and take me back to Hell.

Nick reaches over and snatches up the bottle of lube. "Turn around," he instructs me softly, words barely whispered, thickly coated in evident sexual craving. I oblige, my nerves on high alert, intensely aware that my life is about to do a complete one-eighty.

I'm expecting the cold liquid to coat my ass crack, my puckered hole but I don't expect the gentle touch that caresses between my shoulder blades, running slowly down my spine before landing on my ass cheek.

Tensing involuntarily, I hear the "tsk tsk tsk" coming from Nick. I'm expecting raw and rough so the tenderness I'm experiencing throws me.

Then Nick's mouth is at my ear, his breath tickling my skin before his words drive my lust to unprecedented levels. "I'm going to fuck you within an inch of your life, bring you back and then do it again. Now would be the time to stop me. If not, then hold on for the ride of your life."

Now, I just want him to keep his promise and

"Do it," I say, letting a devilish grin adorn my lips.

In response, I finally feel the cold liquid coating his finger entering my ass. I clench then I relax, letting my lover work his magic. It feels good, and this invasion that I was so brutally taught was evil and unnatural, well I want it and I want it now.

Nick does quick work of sliding a condom onto his dick before he inserts a second finger inside my hole. My cock is throbbing, aching to play, and to feel the friction it was made to have.

The stretching, the prodding and the finger fucks are all accompanied by peppered kisses along my spine meant to soothe me, and they do. Nick's fresh scent envelops me, adding to my relaxed state despite this entirely new experience.

"Spread your legs wide and keep your ass in the air, chest down on the mattress. Don't tense up," he says. The sound of his voice so tranquil, so serene that it does in fact, ease my weary mind.

I do as I'm told and soon I feel the blunt head of Nick's cock prodding my back entrance, my anticipation of pain at an all-time high.

With my forehead pressed against the bed and my ass presented like some kind of medieval offering, I feel two large hands on either of my ass cheeks, spreading and massaging them at once. The action has my body in motion, and my cock instinctively fucking empty air as my ass pushes, back searching for pleasure.

"Here goes," I hear Nick behind me as he pushes in and then pulls his erection out all the while adding more lube to where our bodies are joined.

My hands are gripping the sheets, my body is tense but my mind...fuck, *my mind* is a whirlpool of dirty images flashing like a high-cost porno.

"Just do it," I tell him through gritted teeth. "Just fuck me now."

And then he's in. Nick's dick has finally pushed in through my ring of muscles, and the searing pain has me seeing white spots dancing around my eyes. But it's worth it.

"Holy hell, Brandon, you feel good." Nick is panting, I can sense him holding back, trembling as he fights the primitive instinct to ram his dick far inside me.

So I do it for him.

There's a man's cock buried inside of me and besides the bite of pain that I knew would come, all I know at this moment is total ecstasy. I am full, I am complete, and I am finally...me.

With his hands gripping my hips, his fingers biting into my flesh, I finally...finally, have him where I want him.

Deep inside and to the hilt.

The mattress gives way to Nick's weight on either side of my thighs right before his chest presses against my back, one arm bracing while the other hand reaches around my throat.

Nick is still not thrusting. It's like a torturous wait, this anticipation of getting fucked.

When his breath hits my ear, he tells me, "Turn to face me, Brandon. Kiss me while I fuck you for the first time."

Turning my head, our lips crash together like hurricane waves hitting the Florida shores—fast and devastating.

I'm so concentrated on his talented tongue that I barely register the fact that he is, in fact, pumping his shaft in and out of me. Between his masculine scent, his heated skin and perfectly honed skills, I feel whole for the very first time in my life.

Thrusting slowly at first, our mouths follow the rhythm but soon after, between his hand at my throat, his dick in my ass and his tongue in my mouth, my body is in overdrive.

As our fucking grows more and more erratic, our mouths can barely keep up, the oxygen seriously lacking. But Nick does not back away, he stays close breathing into me, sliding wet lips against wet lips, staring straight into my dark eyes and letting me know a million things without using a single word.

As his free hand reaches around my waist and latches on to my engorged cock I realize that I won't be lasting long this way if he continues. By this point I'm grunting like an animal trying desperately to keep myself from coming too soon.

"Ahhhh, gonna come," he warns me as his hand strokes me harder with more fervent determination and I can feel my time is about up.

Just as we both explode in a blissful eruption of pure ecstasy I grin thinking...I'm gay because this is the only time in my entire life where sex wasn't just a process, it was a need above all others with a pleasure I have never experienced before in my life.

I am gay, and I'm okay with that.

Thank you, Santa. Thank you for stuffing my stocking like nobody's business.

Chapter 5

CHRISTMAS DAY

It's finally here. After all the counting days, preparations, gift buying, gift wrapping, decorating, baking and cooking—-Christmas morning dawns beautiful and peaceful in our town.

The church bells chime, some snowflakes dutifully fall glazing the streets with pure white dazzle, and most everything else is closed for the day.

Even the local Big Mart.

It's Santa's day to rest.

At 7:30 a.m. Sonya Gibbons rolls out of bed, a definite bounce in her step she hasn't had in a long, long time. She hums to herself as she opens a can of cat food for her furry feline roommate, and plugs the coffee pot in. She finds a Christmas tin in her cupboard, and fills it with the homemade gingerbread cookies she baked last night.

Once finished, she finds some bright red ribbon and wraps it around the tin, making a festive bow on top. This Christmas is the first one she hasn't dreaded since her husband left her. She smiles, taking a sip of her coffee laced with cinnamon and thinks about what she'll wear when she drops off her homemade cookies to Santa in Room 232 of the Motel 6.

Oh, she knows their lovemaking was a one-time deal, still she feels inclined to show her gratitude to the Santa Claus who made Christmas magical again for her.

∞

It's a few minutes after 8 a.m. when Libby Daniels picks the last scraps of wrapping paper from the floor of the living room. The kids were up with the chickens, tearing into their gifts, and giving the appropriate squeals of delights, or more obligatory "Thanks Aunt Libby," when they unwrapped socks or underwear.

The church bus had picked them up promptly at 8 for the Christmas services, followed by a potluck breakfast. Libby has her famous breakfast casserole in the oven baking now. She will join them there for breakfast.

She is baking two casseroles as a matter of fact. A smaller one that she plans to drop off at Room 232 of the Motel 6 on her way to their church around ten o'clock.

She hopes Nick likes eggs, sausage, bacon and hash brown potatoes with melted cheese baked to a crusty brown on top. It's her specialty. She owes someone a big thanks for ringing her bell this year, and finally transitioning her into the woman she knew she was.

Thank God for Santa Claus.

∞

Across town, Lacey Stevens has just finished her workout and is taking a quick shower. She and Stacy are expected at their parents to Sunday brunch. It is a tradition, but Lacey is inclined to skip the tradition this year, and implore her twin sister to make excuses for her.

She slips on her prosthesis, fastening the straps securely, and then begins to towel dry her damp locks. She glances over to the wrapped package on her bed and allows a smile to grace her lips. She made a homemade porn video for Santa Nick, and burned a DVD of it to give him. She wants him to remember her every bit as much as she will remember him, and treasure their lusty time spent in his bed. He made this Christmas the very best one she's had since the accident. Lacey's faith in humanity—especially the male variety—has been rekindled because of Santa Nick.

Her thighs clench at the memory of their night together. She hasn't stopped masturbating since then she realizes. Maybe just maybe he'll be open to watching the DVD together . . . and then, well anything could happen right? She won't rule out the possibilities.

Oh. My. Santa.

Brandon zips his jacket up tighter as he heads out to warm up his car. Christmas morning is just as it should be: a sprinkling of snow covers the ground, Jack Frost is nipping playfully at his ass, and he can see his breath as he scrapes some frost from the windshield.

He's up and about earlier than normal but he is on a mission this wonderful Christmas morning. He actually purchased some stocking stuffers for Nick. He knows that Nick will be going back to his real life, his real home now that Christmas is here, but he wouldn't feel right not showing him the gratitude he feels for the Santa who changed his way of thinking. He's never had a better Christmas. A true awakening in every sense of the word.

So Brandon felt it appropriate to buy some special treats for Nick. Flavored lube, sensitizing gel, and a condom sampler pack. Maybe they'd even have time to try a few out?

He glances at his watch and sees that it's about nine-thirty. Perfect time. Check out isn't until noon so plenty of time he thinks as he pulls out onto the street in the direction of the Motel 6.

You better watch out Santa. Brandon is coming for you.

The morning has been a peacefully quiet one for Lorraine Boggs, the first shift desk manager at the Motel 6. Just the way she likes them. It's Christmas. The occupancy rate is down. People are chilling with their families and all is well at the motel. The night shift manager said it was a breeze. She loves days like this when there's no influx of customers, nobody scheduled to check out according to the register on the desk computer. She can relax. Drink coffee and watch some television on the wall mounted flat screen in the lobby.

Piece of cake.

Piece of Christmas cake.

Until just before ten a.m. Then she happens to look out into the parking lot where several cars have pulled in, there occupants getting out with what appears to be Christmas goodies.

Hmm? Party in one of the rooms? Kind of early for that she thinks to herself.

She walks over to the door and peers out. They all seem to be going up to the second floor rooms. They go around the corner and are gone from her sight. She shrugs and goes back behind the counter, filling her coffee mug again.

Several minutes later, a blast of cold air hits her as the same group of people file into the lobby, stomping their feet on the runner by the door. Three chicks and a dude.

"May I help you?" Lorraine asks cordially.

"Hope so," the blonde chick says, ambling up to the counter ahead of the others, "Can you tell us if the gentleman in Room 232 has checked out?"

"Name?" Lorraine asks.

"Umm Nick."

"Last name?" she asks patiently.

She looks around at the others for help. They shrug and look just as bewildered. She turns back around to Lorraine. "He's . . . he's Santa. Drives a black pick-up truck, comes back in a Santa costume. Works over at the Big Mart, you know?"

Lorraine wonders if this gal has been nipping the nog already this morning. She smiles and shakes her head. "Can't say that I've seen a Santa around here."

The guy speaks up. "He's been staying in Room 232 since Thanksgiving."

Now that piece of information is puzzling. They haven't had a long term stay-over all season and that's a fact.

Lorraine goes into the computer and pulls up the registry, going back six weeks. "Folks," she says, looking up from the monitor, "Nobody has been staying in Room 232 since end of October. The roof leaks over that section, and until it's repaired this coming spring, it's vacant, as are the two rooms on either side of it. It's right here on my computer. A work order is still open on it so I don't know what to tell you."

They all glance at one another as if this can't possibly be true.

"But . . . but I was in there just two days ago," the guys says.

"And I was in there last week," one of the ladies' pipes up. "How can this be?"

Lorraine eyes them all cautiously. They don't appear to be stoned or drunk; and they all look well-kept and sane. She believes them. What would be their motivation to lie. Plus, it appears they all came bearing gifts for this non-existent Santa.

"Well," Lorraine says finally, "It's the magic of Santa I guess. Merry Christmas."

And with that:

Merry Christmas to all, and to all a "THE END."

About the Author- Laurel Landon

Former blogger gone self-published author, Laurel Landon is a pen name used for the purpose of keeping my readers and followers in the dark. Since you love taboo and since I love writing it, let's just keep it between us, shall we?

I'm deliciously wicked, some say even a bit twisted, but I blame that on being raised by a witch and a goat in the foothills of Nebraska.

Happy reading!

About The Author - Andrea Smith

ANDREA SMITH IS A USA Today Best-Selling Author of the Alphas In Love Series, along with many others! She has a wicked sense of humor, and no matter the genre, she is able to infuse laughter throughout.

She self-publishes Contemporary Romance, Romantic Suspense, Romantic Comedy, New Adult Romance, MMF Romance, True Crime Fiction and Sensual Romance with a paranormal twist. Many of her books are also available on audio!

Here is a listing of her published fiction to date, an asterisks (*) indicates the book is available on audio!

Maybe Baby Series (New Adult Romance/Suspense)

These Books should be read in order:

Maybe Baby (Book 1)

Baby Love (Book 2)

Be My Baby (Book 3)

Baby Come Back (Book 4)

Men Series (MMF Romance - Should be read in order.)

These Men* (Book 1)

My Men* (Book 2)

Beyond Series (Contemporary Steamy Romance with Paranormal Edge) Can be read as stand-alone, but most enjoyable when read in order.

Broken Promise* (Book 1)

Broken Dreams* (Book 2)

Forbidden Series (New Adult- Taboo - Need to read in order.)

Loving Jesse (Book 1)

Forever Jesse (Book 2)

Black Balled Series (M/M Romance - Need to read in order)

Black Balled* (Book 1)

Guns Blazing* (Book 2)

Hard Edit* (Book 3)

NA Suspense (Stand Alones)

The Preacher

Dirty Diana (releasing Winter 2021)

Wasted (Released, Co-written with Gina A. Jones)

Evermore Series (New Adult Romance - Need to read in order.)

Crushed* (Book 1)

Claimed* (Book 2)

Paparazzi* (Book 3)

Star F*cking* (Book 4)

BBW RomCom

All of Me*

Strictly Business (releasing Winter 2021)

True Crime Fiction

Murders On the Ridge* (Based on the murders of eight family members in Pike County, Ohio)

Do you love audio books which require no membership and are priced reasonably? Check out my audio book store front!

Audio Book Store Front:

https://shop.authors-direct.com/collections/andrea-smith-audio-books

Social Media Links:

To sign up for her monthly newsletter, visit her website: http://www.andreasmithauthor.com/

Follow her on Book Bub:

https://www.bookbub.com/authors/andrea-smith

Follow her on BingeBooks:

https://bingebooks.com/author/andrea-smith

Stalk her on Facebook:

https://www.facebook.com/AndreaSmithAuthor/

GOODREADS:

https://www.goodreads.com/author/show/6869343.Andrea_Smith

INSTAGRAM:

https://www.instagram.com/andreawritesromance/

Follow her on All Author:

https://allauthor.com/profile/andreasmithauthor/

SANTA'S STOCKING STUFFERS

SNEAK PEEK OF STRICTLY BUSINESS

77

Synopsis

TWENTY-FIVE YEAR OLD Brant Taylor has no plans to settle down anytime soon.

He's just now finding his place in Corporate America, on the fast track at his father's company, "Taylor Toys" and his social calendar is overflowing with possibilities. As the Plant Manager, Brant is a key factor in the selection of suitable candidates for employment, including the summer intern program for college students who may want a future with the company.

But when Brant is forced to hire his younger sister and her friend in the summer intern program, his extra-curricular activities are curtailed due to their antics which seriously push his limit and he's none too happy about it.

His sister's friend, Delilah Mayfield, F.K.A. "Pudge," has some mouth on her he discovers! Typically she is nowhere near the type of girl to pose a distraction for Brant - he prefers them svelte and sweet, and Delilah is neither of those things. Still he finds her a distraction he just doesn't need.

Chapter 1

THE PRODUCTION FLOOR was buzzing away. Every line was up and running and I had no doubt we would meet our production numbers for month end. Six days to go, and the gods permitting, Taylor Toys would set an all-time record for the month of May. June, July and August would be a cinch with the college interns hitting the payroll at lower wages, bringing the profit margins up even further as no overtime would be needed. Cheap labor would fill-in for the permanent workers taking their vacations here and there, and keep productivity high.

The old man would be jizzing himself at the end of the third quarter. He'd know for sure that all the money shelled out for my Ivy League education had been worth every well-squeezed nickel of his.

You have to understand. My father at sixty-seven should be enjoying Baby Boomer retirement. But no, not him. He's not quite ready to pass the torch until he's sure his eldest child has been properly molded into his idea of the perfect President and C.E.O. for Taylor Toys. I love my old man, I really do, but he's got to shed some of the "don't fix it if it ain't broke" mentality. I have bigger plans for expansion of Taylor Toys. And I haven't actually sprang it on him just yet You know what they say: *timing is everything!*

Let me back up just a little so you can get a better picture. My mother, who is fifteen years younger than Dad, blessed him with two children when he was well into his forties.

As the oldest child at twenty-five, I was well tutored in Dad's toy business from the time I was sixteen and started working summers there, continuing that routine through my college years.

Dad always used to say, "Brant, someday this could be all yours, son. Just as my father, your late grandfather, Jedidiah B. (for Brant) Taylor passed on to me, once he was sure that I'd keep the high quality standards, and moral principles that made Taylor Toys the most respected and profitable mid-size company in the industry.

"We aren't Hasbro or Mattel, son, but then we don't aspire to be them. You see, unlike the 'big names' who outsource most of their components to low cost economies, Taylor Toys' prides themselves on having all of their components made and assembled in the USA. Remember that, Brant. Source and manufacture domestically, sell globally. It's the American way, boy."

I knew Dad had lived by that mantra, but in the age of globalization, it was difficult at times to source parts domestically for the purpose of keeping material costs down so the finished products could be marketed competitively, and attain the best profit margins. When I had told Dad this once I came on board full-time after college, as the Supply Chain Manager, he'd put up a bit of a fuss.

"Brant," he said in that educational tone, "I don't answer to stockholders, son. I don't have to price the goods to match those competitors. What Taylor Toys offers, and has always offered, are good quality toys, designed and developed right here."

"But Dad," I argued, "While you may not answer to stockholders, you are a 'for-profit,' business, right? The least you can do is let me open a project on it for comparison purposes."

He caved (like I knew he would) and gave me the go-ahead to put together a project, costing out every component of our three best-selling products. They all happened to be dolls, of course.

The Bambino Alive Doll Line was our top seller. These babies ranged from newborn to toddler, males and females, Caucasian, African-American, Asian, and Hispanic. The dolls ate, peed, pooped and puked.

I know, right? Top sellers globally. Go figure.

The second best-selling line was the Puberty Pals. You got it, the dolls in this line were considered *educational*. They were used in schools to assist in teaching Health and Sex Education classes. They weren't sold at retail outlets.

The third best-selling line was my personal favorite. It was the "Babes in Boyland" line. That was about as sexy as it got at Taylor Toys. These were the typical 11.5" dolls which I had computed using 1/6 scale in real life would be a 5'9" female with measurements of 36-18-33. Does it get any sexier than that? Can you picture this chick? Legs all the way up to her neck for Chrissake.

Get hold of yourself, Brant.

Back to the topic. These dolls competed with the age old Barbie/Ken scenario, and we did all of the flavors as well. Our marketing and design groups were always at work planning novel, limited edition releases for collectors around Christmas and Hanukkah time.

Lest I put you to sleep with all of this, let me jump to the crux. Through price/cost analysis, I determined that if Taylor Toys wanted to remain a *source domestic parts only'* toy manufacturer, and still remain competitive in the global market, we needed to do our own injection molding.

So, Taylor Toys' Manufacturing Engineers got busy and presented my father with a capital expense project to add on an injection molding department at a cost of $1.4 million. With a three year ROI payback.

My father's words to me: "Son, you better hope I don't regret approving this Capex. Your future depends upon it."

So, how's *that* for pressure?

As a bonus, I was promoted to Plant Manager, so I could personally over-see Production, Supply Chain, and the factory support offices.

I reported directly to my old man who was still acting Operations Manager across the street at the Ivory Tower. (That's what we *shop rats* coined the main offices) My father's office was located there because he was keen on keeping a close eye on the Accounting, Marketing, and Purchasing Departments. As he often told me, "Those are the folks making, spending and counting my money, so I gotta make sure they see my presence each and every day, son." As you can see, my father still had his hand tightly clutched on the pulse of the company.

For now.

But I was the heir apparent, so was it any wonder I worked my ass off to make sure that happened? And did I mention how it had seriously impacted my social life? There were so many unhappy and unfulfilled women now settling for less in the greater Des Moines, Iowa area. Never let it be said that Brant J. (for Jedidiah) Taylor did not have his priorities in order! Yeah, my friends called me B.J., and I didn't object that much!

Just as I was checking the production count off of Press #2 for first shift, I heard the shrill hum of the PA system alerting the shop floor that a page was coming across. Maggie Campbell, the Human Resources Manager's tentative voice came across the speakers:

"Brant Taylor, please report to Conference Room 1. Brant Taylor to Conference Room 1."

I glanced at my watch. It was ten minutes after three. My smart watch evidently hadn't given me a warning; of course, it might have helped if I had programmed the meeting in for today. My bad. My old man was likely already there, getting ready for his typical welcome speech to the summer interns.

Luckily most of them of them would be returns from previous summer internships as they edged up another year in their college degree program.

The rookies were the hand-picked college freshmen with no previous experience at Taylor Toys. Often a cocky bunch, the rookies were always the biggest pain in the ass until they were properly broken in. Their summer internships would likely make them yearn for fall semester to start, or maybe propel them into changing their majors. We mostly recruited Business, Marketing or Engineering majors for the program.

And yes, I had been put in charge of the rookies since some of them would actually be put on the production floor. I would be blessed with ten of them. I would screen their abilities and right off the bat; I knew one of them would test my restraint.

That's right. My younger sister Brooke had just finished her sophomore year at Carnegie Mellon in Pittsburgh, majoring in Marketing. Hopefully, Maggie would assign Brooke to some paper-pushing job over in the Ivory Tower. I loved my sister, don't get me wrong, but I also *knew* my sister.

Spoiled seven ways from Sunday, I could only imagine the meltdown it would cause should she break a nail performing some mundane task in the factory. Nope. I just couldn't see it.

I pushed open the door to Conference Room #1 which was just off the assembly floor, pulling off my safety glasses and tossing them onto the conference room table.

"Sorry about that," I apologized, not really looking at the fifteen or so interns sitting around the large, oblong table.

My father was standing up front behind the wooden podium, and gave me a nod. "Glad you could make it, Brant. Switch off the lights please, I want to get this overview started."

Not overly pissed. It was the same scenario each year. Dad would present a power point presentation showing the history of the company, the various products manufactured here, and the happy, smiling and productive faces of the employees here at Taylor Toys.

I switched off the lights, and sat back as he started the spiel. It was a fifteen minute presentation which I knew by heart.

At about seven minutes into it, I heard the sounds of soft snickering. Yep, it always happened when the presentation focused on the 'Puberty Pal' doll line. For shit's sake, you'd think this was an audience of nine year olds, not *nine-teen and twenty year olds!* As if the guys hadn't seen pussy, or the chicks hadn't fondled a guys junk yet.

"Look at that one's teeny-weenie," a female voice whispered to whoever was sitting beside her. *"Right? Just like Josh's dick,"* the other female voice whispered back, sounding very much like *my* sister. And who the hell was Josh?

"Shhh," someone at the table hissed. Of course, the old man hadn't heard any of it. It was selective hearing, although he claimed it was his age. I didn't buy it. He knew Brooke. And nothing she said or did was ever wrong. He continued on and there weren't any further distractions.

Finally I heard him say, "Lights," and I flipped the switch to illuminate the overhead lighting.

"Well, now that you've learned a little something about Taylor Toys, are there any questions?" he asked, looking around.

There was stony silence, and nobody raised a hand or called out. That was fairly typical as well. Maggie and I would be bombarded with questions once Dad left the conference room and we began the introductions and assignments. The questions of course would be typical of the rookie mentality:

How much is the hourly wage?

How long is our lunch break?

Can we pick our shift?

Do we get sick pay?

Do you pay medical and dental?

Can I have a job where I'm not standing all day?

"Well then, if there are no questions, I will leave you in the capable hands of our Director of Human Resources, Maggie

Campbell, along with Brant Taylor, the Plant Manager. Welcome to the Taylor Toy family."

He left the conference room, giving me a nod and a smile as he did so. Maggie went up to the podium, a stack of files in her hands.

"Welcome everyone to our Summer Intern Program here at Taylor Toys. This is such a fantastic opportunity for all of you to experience various aspects of the design, manufacturing, marketing and international business platforms in a hands-on manner. You will be a part of the process, and hopefully, the experience will lend itself in channeling your focus on the career path you wish to take after graduation.

"I've reviewed all of your files, and have done my best to match your course of study with the intern positions we have open for the summer. So, at this point in time, I'd like to read off the names of those who will be placed across the street in our main offices. When I call your name, please come up and get your orientation folder which contains the job description, hours, and name of the direct supervisor you will be reporting to. Once I've called those of you selected for office positions, I will escort you over there and Brant will assign the rest of you to positions here."

Fuck. I hoped like hell Maggie was assigning Brooke to the main office. I hadn't had a chance to specifically make that request, but common sense would dictate it would be better my entitled sister not be placed under my authority one would think, right?

Apparently not.

"Neil Schindler, you are assigned to Accounts Payable."

"David Adams, you will be placed in Design Engineering."

"Melissa Grant, it's Marketing for you."

"Carey Justice, Human Resources with me as your mentor. Congratulations."

"Jeb Sandler, you're assigned to Purchasing."

"Victoria Simms, you will be helping in Accounts Receivable."

I watched as one by one the apparent cream of the crop was called to go across the street to the ivory tower. I guess that really wasn't fair because I had no clue about the ten interns Maggie left for me. I looked around, seeing the smirk on Brooke's face as she batted her eyelashes at me in feigned innocence. What was up with her? I would've bet she'd sweet talked Dad into getting something cushy in the office. Maybe she wanted to torment me.

"Uh, excuse me, Mrs. Campbell," I called out as she started to leave the podium. "Can I talk to you for just a moment?"

She glanced at the group she was taking over to the Ivory Tower, "Wait outside for me, please. I'll be right with you." They did as instructed and she turned her attention back to me. "Yes, Brant?"

"It's just that Brooke Taylor is majoring in Marketing. I would think she'd be a better fit in that department. Would you consider switching Brooke out with Melissa Grant?" I asked, giving her one of my signature smiles.

I could tell Maggie didn't like being second-guessed, but what the fuck? It made perfect sense to me. She gave me a gratuitous smile. "Brooke specifically requested a position in manufacturing. She felt in order to market a product, you must first understand the product. I think that's a crucial point, don't you agree?"

"Uh, yeah sure," I replied, coming off as a dumbass instead of the freakin' plant manager of this operation. Apparently Brooke assumed Dad was going to oust the current Director of Marketing to put her in the slot in three years.

"Glad you agree," Maggie replied, "Oh, and I left the roster of the ten interns you get to keep, along with some recommendations, but of course, the ultimate decision is yours, Brant. Good luck."

And with that, she whisked out the door leaving me with my rookies. I took my place behind the podium, and glanced out at the ten interns left, sitting around the table. Three chicks, seven dudes.

My sister had a shit-eating grin going on most likely due to the fact she felt she'd gotten one over on her older brother. I just knew she'd be testing my authority all damn summer. And that's when I saw *her.* Sitting next to Brooke, fidgeting with her hair, and giving me a big wide grin.

I glanced quickly down at my roster to be sure. No way!

But there it was. Her name.

Delilah Mayfield.

I looked back up quickly, and before I could put any thought into it, insert my politically correct filter, I blurted out the nickname I'd given her years back.

"Pudge?"

Did you love *Santa's Stocking Stuffers*? Then you should read *Blacklisted*[1] by Andrea Smith!

[2]

Two dominant males, two worthy adversaries, in a business that takes no prisoners, will soon learn that fate refuses to be ignored . . . My name is Troy Babilonia, but I'm best known as Babu, a renowned literary critic with my own online column. I'm followed by thousands! I'm a living god in the literary world. I have no filter, and for that, my flock of humble followers are forever grateful. If it weren't for me, they wouldn't know what to read. I have zero tolerance for the weak-minded attention seekers, nor do I have respect for the self-proclaimed

---

1. https://books2read.com/u/mvnZaj

2. https://books2read.com/u/mvnZaj

geniuses of the Indie world. My advice to all Indie authors is to never break the cardinal rule in this cut-throat business. Ever. ***My name is L. Blackburn*** and I'm an Indie author. My extraordinary genius was loved and worshiped throughout the literary world, until one egocentric critic tried to obliterate my career. It seems I broke some "cardinal rule," and now I'm paying the price for it. But I don't plan on going down without a fight.

"Bring it, Babu!"

Sexual Content. M/M - Graphic Sexual Situations

(Previously published as "Black Balled")

Read more at www.andreasmithauthor.com.

Also by Andrea Smith

ALPHAS IN LOVE
Slate
Trace
Easton
Cruisin' With the G-Men
Taz
Weston
Bryce

Beyond Series
Broken Dreams

Dream Series
Shadows & Dreams
These Dreams
Shattered Dreams
Dream Lover

Evermore Series
Crushed
Claimed
Paparazzi
Star F*cking

G-Man
Carson: The Untold Story

Limbo
Silent Whisper
Stolen Dreams

M/M ALPHAS
Blacklisted
Quid Pro Quo

MMF Sandwich
Triple Play
Double Header
My Men Duet

Naughty Nuggets
Santa's Stocking Stuffers

Standalone
Southern Comfort
Dream Series Box Set
Murders On The Ridge
Bitch Games: We All Play Them
The Other Man
Wasted
Hard Balled
All of Me
Maybe Baby Box Set
Love in Limbo Anthology

Watch for more at www.andreasmithauthor.com.

Also by Laurel Landon

Naughty Nuggets
Santa's Stocking Stuffers